Bear at Work
Oso en el trabajo

Stella Blackstone
Debbie Harter

POST OFFICE • OFICINA DE CORREOS

Barefoot Books
step inside a story

Bear at work is as busy as can be,
bringing lots of surprises to you and to me.

Oso en el trabajo está muy ocupado,
trayendo muchas sorpresas para ti y para mí.

**He has postcards for the florist
and letters for the baker.**

Él tiene postales para la florista
y cartas para el panadero.

He has boxes for the corner shop
that sells the morning papers.

Él tiene cajas para la tienda de la esquina
que vende los periódicos matinales.

He strides past every house and home,
stopping here and there.

Él pasa por cada casa y hogar,
parando aquí y allá.

He brings books to the librarian
across the market square.

Él lleva unos libros al bibliotecario
que está frente al mercado.

**He steps inside the café,
where he has a cup of tea.**

Él entra al café,
donde toma una taza de té.

At the school, he gives a package
to the children in Room Three.

En la escuela, él entrega un paquete
a los niños del salón tres.

**He has letters for the farmer,
who has recently been wed.**

Él tiene cartas para el granjero,
quien se ha **casado** **recientemento**.

He even has a present for
the little bear in bed.

Él incluso tiene un regalo para
el osito que está en cama.

Bear's sack is empty; his day is done.
Being a postman is lots of fun.

El saco de Oso está vacío; su día ha terminado.
Ser cartero es muy divertido.

Bears at Work

Can you spot these working bears in the story?
What would you like to do when you grow up?

florist
la florista

baker
el panadero

shopkeeper
la tendera

builder
el constructor

librarian
el bibliotecario

Osos en el trabajo

¿Ves a estos osos trabajadores en el cuento?
¿Qué te gustaría ser cuando seas mayor?

waitress
la mesera

teacher
el maestro

farmer
el granjero

doctor
la doctora

postman
el cartero

Vocabulary / Vocabulario

post office – la oficina de correos
flower shop – la floristería
bakery – la panadería
newsstand – el quiosco
house – la casa
library – la biblioteca
café – el café
school – la escuela
farm – la granja
hospital – el hospital
my home – mi hogar

Barefoot Books
2067 Massachusetts Ave
Cambridge, MA 02140

Barefoot Books
29/30 Fitzroy Square
London, W1T 6LQ

Text copyright © 2008 by Stella Blackstone
Illustrations copyright © 2008 by Debbie Harter
The moral rights of Stella Blackstone and
Debbie Harter have been asserted

First published in Great Britain by Barefoot Books, Ltd
and in the United States of America by Barefoot Books, Inc in 2008
This bilingual Spanish edition first published in 2012
All rights reserved

Graphic design by Barefoot Books, Oxford and
Louise Millar, London Reproduction by Grafiscan, Verona
Printed in China on 100% acid-free paper
This book was typeset in Futura and Slappy
The illustrations were prepared in paint, pen and ink, and crayon

ISBN 978-1-84686-769-9

British Cataloguing-in-Publication Data:
a catalogue record for this book is available from the British Library

Library of Congress Cataloging-in-Publication Data
is available upon request

Translator: María A. Pérez

3 5 7 9 8 6 4